AALFRED AND AALBERT

MORAG HOOD

TW🦉 HOOTS

This is the story of two aardvarks.

I'm Aalfred,

thought Aalfred.

FOR MISHA AND KIYO,
THE AARDVARKS WHO INSPIRED THIS STORY.

First published 2019 by Two Hoots
an imprint of Pan Macmillan
20 New Wharf Road, London N1 9RR
Associated companies throughout the world
www.panmacmillan.com
ISBN 978-1-5098-4294-0
Text and illustrations copyright © Morag Hood 2019
Moral rights asserted.

1 3 5 7 9 8 6 4 2
A CIP catalogue record for this book is available from the British Library.
Printed in China
The illustrations in this book were painted in gouache and then digitally coloured.

www.twohootsbooks.com

Aalfred loved stars, broccoli and picnics.

Aalbert loved flowers, sunshine and cheese.

And they both loved sleeping
rather a lot, except . . .

Aalbert slept all night,

and Aalfred slept all day.

Which meant that they
had never met each other.

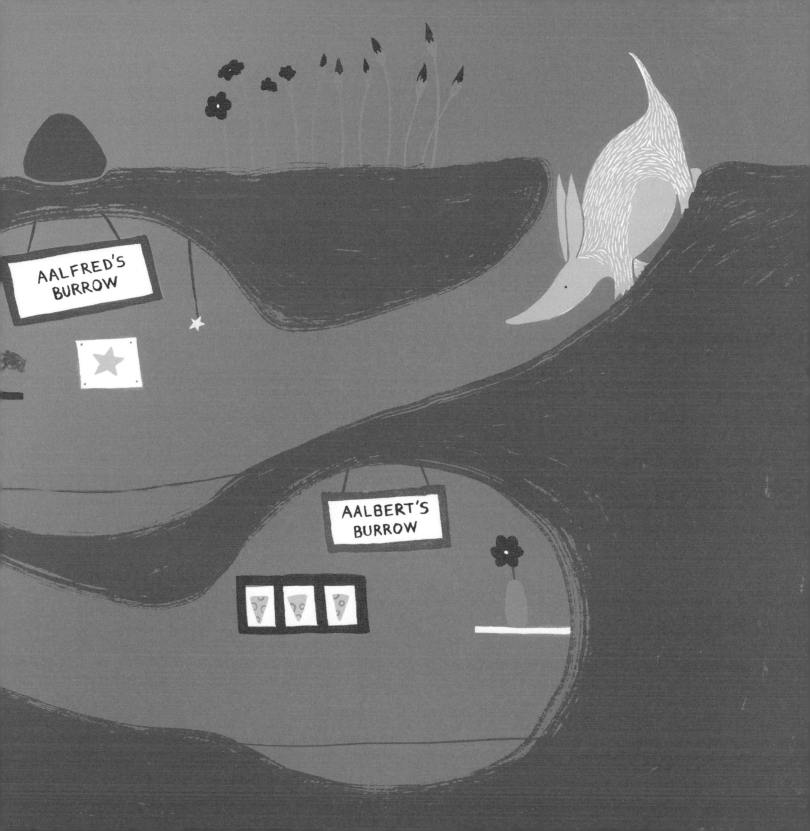

. . . or one of a two,

thought Aalbert.

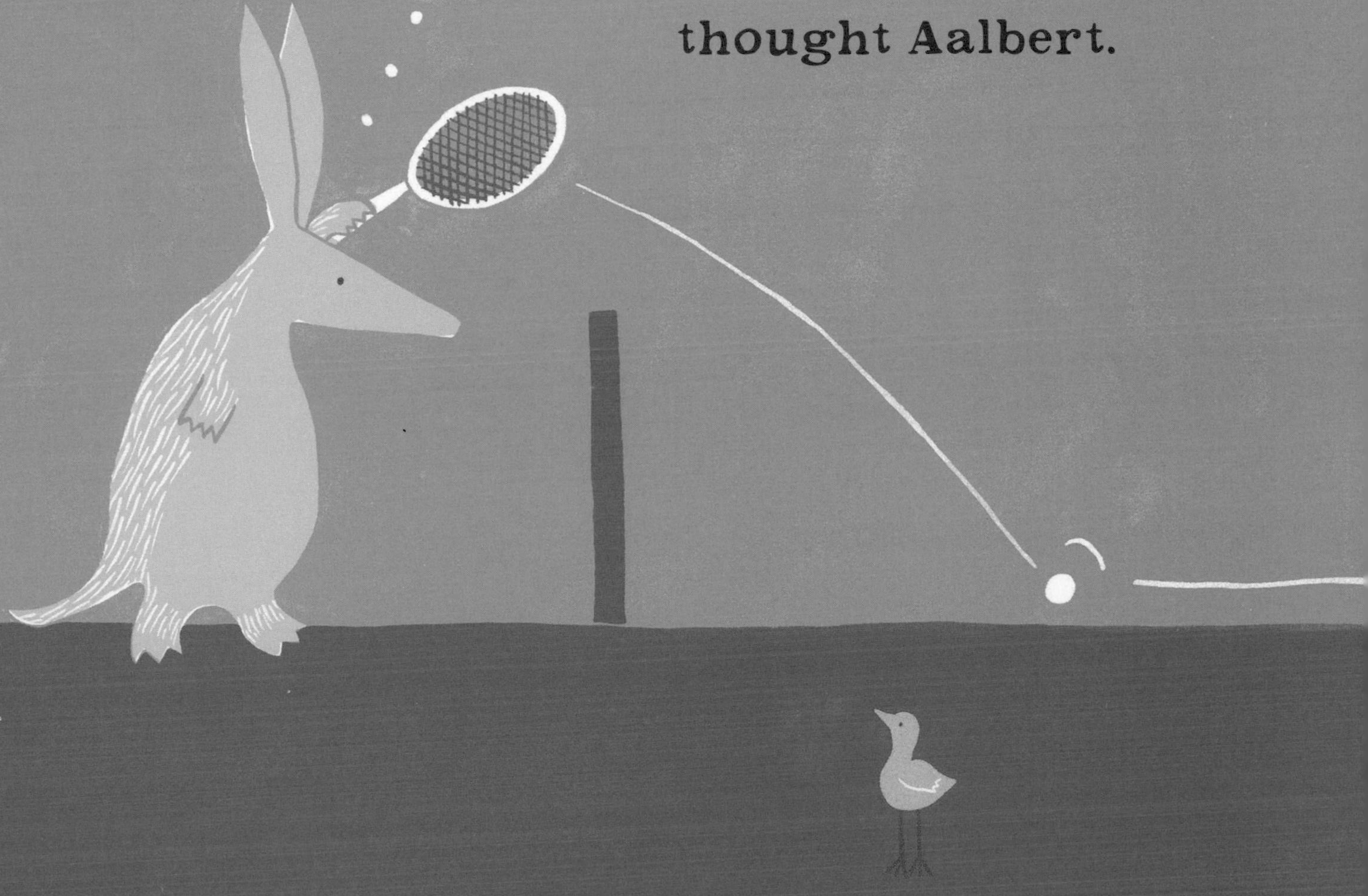

But most of the time their minds
were on other things.

Unless . . .

. . . somebody came up with a plan.

But nothing changed when Aalbert
was woken up one night.

thought Aalbert . . .

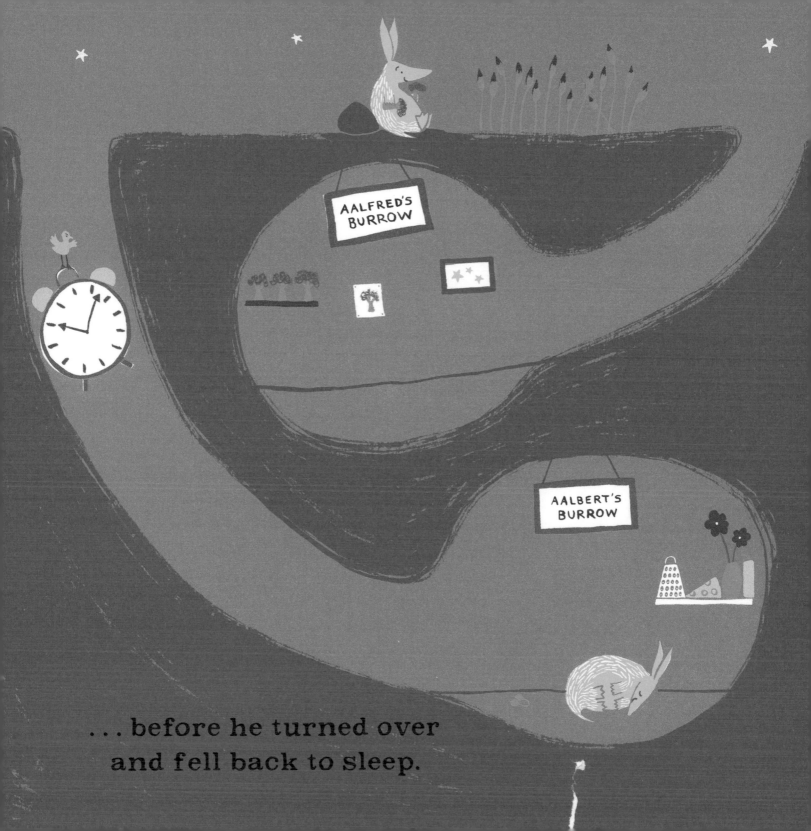

AALFRED'S BURROW

AALBERT'S BURROW

... before he turned over
and fell back to sleep.

Nothing changed when Aalfred
saw something very unusual.

I wonder
where that
broccoli is
going?

thought Aalfred ...

... before he carried
on with his evening.

Nothing changed even when they both
got in a bit of a tangle.

It seemed that nothing could bring
Aalfred and Aalbert together.

Nothing at all.

And that was very sad.

I know how to cheer that bird up!

thought Aalfred.

And,

in a way,

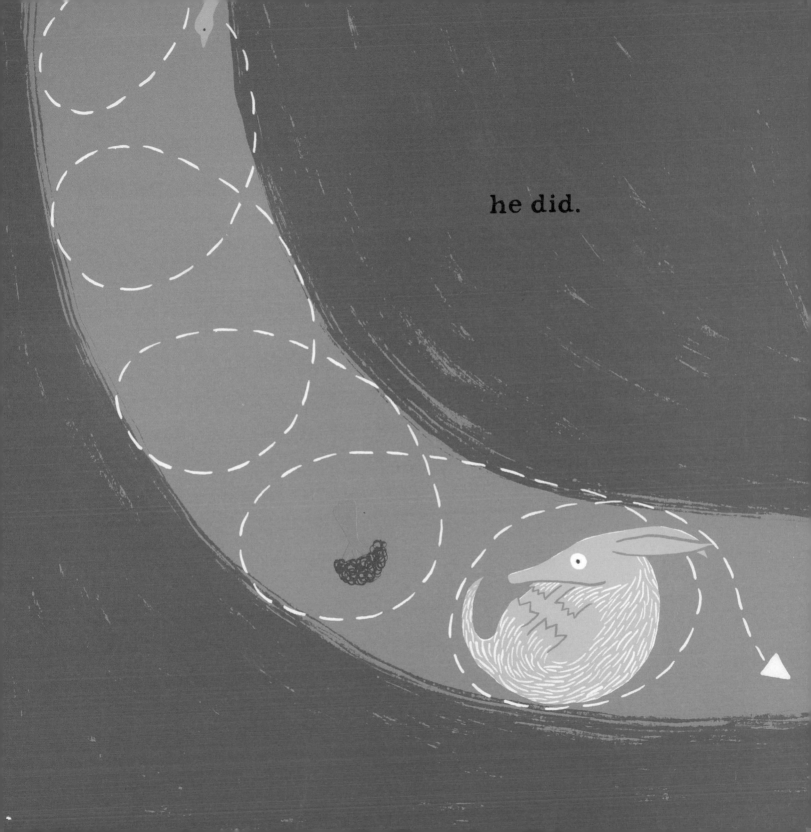

he did.

**Because that was the story of
how Aalfred met Aalbert ...**

And they all lived happily ever aafter.